DRAGON MASTERS

WAVE OF THE SEA DRAGON

BY

TRACEY WEST

BRANCHES

SCHOLASTIC INC.

DRAGON MASTERS

➤ Read All the Adventures ➤

More books coming soon!

TABLE OF CONTENTS

THANK YOU TO BERNIDA WEBB-BINDER,

for sharing her expertise on the art and history
of the Pacific Islands. — TW

Library of Congress Cataloging-in-Publication Data
Names: West, Tracey, 1965- author. | Loveridge, Matt, illustrator.
Title: Wave of the sea dragon / by Tracey West ; [illustrated by Matt Loveridge]
Description: First edition. | New York : Branches/Scholastic Inc., 2021. | Series: Dragon masters ; 19 |
Audience: Ages 5-7. | Audience: Grades 2-3. | Summary: Drake and the other Dragon Masters go to the island of Kapua seeking a Sea Dragon needed to help stop the evil wizard Astrid's dangerous False Life spell.
Identifiers: LCCN 2020024279 (print) | LCCN 2020024280 (ebook) | ISBN 9781338635485 (paperback) |
ISBN 9781338635492 (library binding) | ISBN 9781338635508 (ebook)
Subjects: CYAC: Dragons—Fiction. | Magic—Fiction. | Wizards—Fiction. |
Adventure and adventurers—Fiction.
Classification: LCC PZ7.W51937 Wav 2021 (print) | LCC PZ7.W51937 (ebook) | DDC [Fic]—dc23
LC record available at https://lccn.loc.gov/2020024279
LC ebook record available at https://lccn.loc.gov/2020024280

10 9 8 7 6 5 4 3 2 1   21 22 23 24 25

Printed in China   62

First edition, July 2021
Illustrated by Matt Loveridge
Edited by Katie Carella
Book design by Sarah Dvojack

THE WIZARD
IN THE BUBBLE

Worm, take us inside the Fortress of the Stone Dragon!" Drake yelled.

Drake heard the other Dragon Masters gasp. His Earth Dragon, Worm, glowed bright green. Then Drake and Worm disappeared from King Roland's castle before anyone could stop them.

1

Worm transported them to the fortress in just a few seconds. But in those few seconds, Drake had a lot of thoughts.

Astrid

Jayana, the Head Wizard, had just told Drake and the other Dragon Masters they were too late — Astrid was about to cast the False Life spell!

Astrid was an evil wizard. She planned to use the spell on the bones of giant ancient beasts. She wanted to bring the creatures to life to help her take over the world.

The wizards couldn't get close enough to stop Astrid. She had cast many powerful defense spells to keep wizards out of the fortress.

Dragons might be able to get past the spells. But the wizards didn't want the Dragon Masters to try to stop Astrid. They all said it was too dangerous.

I know it's dangerous, Drake thought. *But I have to try!*

Drake's mind raced as his dragon's green light faded. *Will Astrid be waiting for us?* he wondered. *Will she hit us with magic as soon as we get there?*

They landed in the main courtyard of the Fortress of the Stone Dragon.

We did it! Drake thought. *Worm and I made it past Astrid's defense spells with no problem.*

Drake did not see Astrid. But he saw his friends. Caspar and his Stone Dragon, Shaka, looked like gray stone statues. So did Mina and her Ice Dragon, Frost.

Drake, Caspar, Mina, and their dragons had tried to stop Astrid before. She had turned them all — except Drake — into stone. Worm had found a way to break free, but the others were still statues.

Drake almost started to cry, but he stopped himself.

If I can stop Astrid, the wizards can save them, he thought.

Then he spoke to Worm. "Can you sense Astrid? Where is she?" he whispered.

Drake's Dragon Stone glowed as he heard Worm's voice inside his head.

She is in the Garden of the Beasts.

They slowly walked across the courtyard. The tall stone walls of the fortress rose high above them. Drake and Worm kept close to the walls so Astrid wouldn't see them coming.

Drake tiptoed to the opening that led to the Garden of the Beasts. His heart beat quickly as he peered inside. Enormous bones were scattered across the sand. Astrid floated in the air inside a red bubble. Her legs were crossed, and her eyes were closed.

The bubble hung in the air over a wide, flat rock. On top of the rock, Drake saw the spell ingredients. One mandrake root. A branch from a shadow bush. The tail feather of a ghost raven. A sprig of black mistletoe. And the tooth of a spirit bear.

She cannot cast the spell without all five ingredients, Drake thought. *So if I can steal even one of them, I can stop her!*

MY SPELL!

rake spoke to Worm inside his head so Astrid wouldn't hear.

It looks like Astrid is in a trance. She must be starting to cast the spell! I'll sneak up and steal as many of the ingredients as I can, Drake said. *Watch Astrid. Warn me if she opens her eyes.*

Be careful, Drake, Worm replied.

Drake nodded.

He ran into the Garden of the Beasts. He dashed toward the flat stone. Astrid's bubble floated over his head.

He reached out to grab the ingredients. Before he could touch anything, he heard Worm's voice in his head:

Drake, we've got to leave now!

Drake grabbed what he could — the branch of thorns.

Green light flashed as Worm transported into the Garden of the Beasts.

Then Drake heard a shriek above him.
"MY SPELL!"

He looked up to see the bubble pop. Still floating in the air, Astrid pointed a finger at Drake. Sparks sizzled on her fingertip. "You and your dragon will not get away from me again!" she yelled.

DON'T TOUCH THE THORNS!

Drake dived and touched Worm's tail with his free hand.

"To Bracken, Worm!" Drake yelled.

Whoosh! Worm transported them away.

Drake blinked. He and Worm were back in the underground Training Room in Bracken Castle.

"You shouldn't have gone to the fortress by yourself, Drake," scolded Griffith. The white-haired wizard trained Drake and all of King Roland's Dragon Masters.

"Astrid could have done something terrible to you," said Jayana.

Dragon Masters Rori, Ana, and Bo ran up to Drake. Eko the Dragon Mage followed them. Behind them stood the new Dragon Master, Opeli, with her Lava Dragon, Ka. Opeli's eyes were wide.

Ana hugged Drake. "I'm so glad you're safe!"

"Wow, Drake, you didn't listen to Griffith," Rori said. "That's something *I* would do."

"I wanted to stop Astrid from casting the spell," he told everyone. "Worm and I transported right into the fortress. I tried to steal the spell ingredients. But all I got was this." He held up the branch from the shadow bush, which was dotted with sharp thorns.

"Be careful with that, Drake!" Jayana warned. "Don't prick yourself."

"What would happen?" Bo asked.

"If you prick yourself with a thorn, you become a shadow," she explained. "That is why it's called a shadow bush."

"And unless you prick yourself a second time within the hour," Griffith added, "you will stay a shadow forever."

"I'll be careful," Drake promised. "Can Astrid cast the spell without the branch?"

Griffith stroked his beard. "No. She needs all five ingredients."

Drake sighed with relief. "Then I'm glad Worm and I went to the fortress," he said. "Maybe it was wrong. But at least we stopped her!"

"Can't she get another branch?" Eko asked.

"The branch must be taken on the night of a full moon," Jayana replied. "That is more than two weeks away."

"That's good news," Drake said. "Two weeks gives us plenty of time to find a Sea Dragon and a Wind Dragon."

Ana had found a way to reverse the False Life spell. The powers of three special dragons were needed to break the spell.

Drake and Ana had already found the first dragon: a Lava Dragon. Now the Dragon Masters needed to find a Sea Dragon and a Wind Dragon.

"Think, Drake," Griffith said. "Does Astrid know where you transported to?"

"I don't —" Drake began, but then he stopped. His mind replayed his escape from the fortress.

"To Bracken, Worm!" he had yelled.

"I think she knows," Drake admitted.

Griffith frowned. "Then we must prepare," he said. "Astrid will not wait two weeks. She will come here soon, looking for that!"

He pointed to the branch in Drake's hand.

KEEP IT SAFE

will find some wizards who can help protect the castle," Jayana said. She snapped her fingers and disappeared.

"Should we ask King Roland's soldiers to guard the branch?" Ana asked.

Drake shook his head. "I've seen Astrid use dark magic to control soldiers. It's safer with us."

Griffith clapped his hands. "Here is what we must do," he said. "Bo has found a Sea Dragon on the island of Kapua. Drake, you shall go to Kapua to find the Sea Dragon. Bring the branch with you. Astrid will not look for you there."

"Griffith, I read one story about Sea Dragons and Lava Dragons. It says they all used to live on the islands of Noa, where Opeli is from," Bo said. "I think Opeli and Ka should go on this mission. Maybe the Sea Dragon will be happy to see Ka."

Opeli looked up at her orange Lava Dragon and nodded. "Yes! Kapua is far from our islands. It will be exciting to go there."

"Excellent plan!" Griffith said. "Bo, you and Shu shall go, too."

"Ana and I will stay and protect the castle," Rori said.

"And we'll try to find out where the Wind Dragon is," Ana added.

Bo ran off. "I will get Shu!" he said.

Griffith handed Drake a map. "This is where you will find the Sea Dragon," he said.

Drake showed the map to Worm. "Got it?" he asked.

Worm nodded. *Yes.*

Drake tucked the map and the branch into his pocket. His hand brushed against his magic mirror. The mirror let him communicate with Griffith from far away.

Bo walked back into the Training Room with a blue dragon with shimmering scales.

"Drake, please ask Worm to transport you all right away," Griffith said. "Return here with the Sea Dragon. This is our best chance to stop Astrid!"

Drake, Bo, and Opeli touched Worm. Bo and Opeli each put a hand on their dragons. Worm transported them all in a flash of green light.

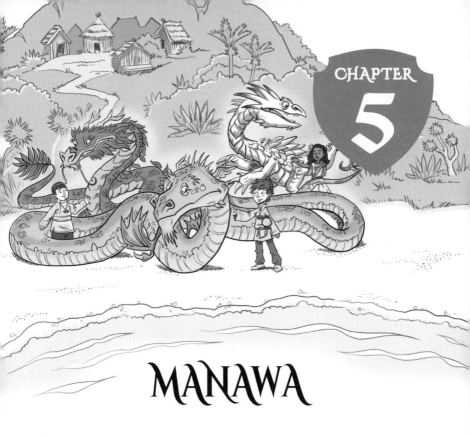

MANAWA

he smell of salt water hit Drake's nose. They had landed on a sandy beach.

They were in a cove shaped like a half circle. Drake noticed plants he'd never seen before. There were tall trees with skinny trunks, and bushes with purple flowers. A hill rose up behind them, and Drake saw the straw-colored roofs of homes there.

"This place reminds me of my island," Opeli remarked.

Bo looked around. "I do not see a Sea Dragon or a Dragon Master," he said.

"A Dragon Master? Is that someone who connects with a dragon?" a voice asked.

A young girl stepped out from the trees. She wore a light-colored shirt and a skirt made of grassy fibers. She had dark, wavy hair.

"Yes," Drake replied. "That's what we are. We're Dragon Masters. I'm Drake, and this is Bo and Opeli. And these are our dragons — Worm, Shu, and Ka."

"My name is Pania," the girl said.

"You're not afraid of dragons?" Opeli asked.

Pania smiled. "Why would I be afraid of baby dragons like yours? They're so cute!"

"Our dragons aren't babies," Drake said. "And we are here on an important mission. We're looking for the Dragon Master of a Sea Dragon. Can you help us?"

"Yes!" Pania said. "You need my brother, Manawa. Follow me."

They followed Pania along the shore and across the cove.

A boy their age stood on top of a boulder with his hands on his hips. He wore a skirt like the one his sister wore, and his curly dark hair was streaked by the sun. Around his neck, he wore a green stone. It looked like an Ahi Stone — the same stone Opeli wore.

"Brother!" the girl called out. "Meet Drake, Bo, and Opeli."

"Hello!" Manawa called back. "What brings you here with your baby dragons?"

Why do they think our dragons are babies? Drake wondered. He wanted to ask, but there were more important things to do.

"An evil wizard is casting a dangerous spell," Drake replied. "We need a Sea Dragon to help us stop it. Your sister told us that you are a Dragon Master."

Manawa jumped down from the boulder. "Dragon Master? That sounds very important," he said. "I was chosen to connect with Tani. But I am not called her Dragon Master. Here, I am called a Dragon Friend."

"I think they mean the same thing," Bo said.

Opeli stepped forward. "You wear an Ahi Stone, like mine."

Manawa nodded. "Yes. It helps me communicate with my dragon."

"Where is your dragon?" Drake asked.

Manawa touched his Ahi Stone. It began to glow.

"Tani, come meet our new friends!" Manawa cried.

ENEMIES, NOT FRIENDS

The calm ocean water began to move. Waves kicked up and slammed against the shore. A huge dragon head rose from the water. Tani looked at them with enormous, green eyes. Red, orange, and yellow fins grew out of the sides of her head.

"Wow!" Opeli exclaimed. "Tani is such a beautiful dragon!"

Tani's body came out of the water. Orange and red scales covered her back. Her belly was smooth and white.

Drake gasped. The Sea Dragon was at least twice as big as Worm, Shu, or Ka!

Manawa turned to his sister. "Pania, go to the village and tell everyone about our visitors," he said. "I will find out more about this evil wizard Drake told us about."

"Yes, Manawa!" Pania ran off.

Manawa's Ahi Stone glowed. "Tani would like to get a better look at your baby dragons," he said.

Drake smiled, shaking his head. "Our dragons aren't babies. They are just smaller than Tani. This is my Earth Dragon, Worm."

"And this is my Water Dragon, Shu," Bo said.

Shu floated through the air up to Tani. The Sea Dragon playfully squirted water through her nose at Shu, who then dipped her tail into the sea and splashed some water at Tani.

"I think they like each other," Bo said, smiling.

Then Opeli and Ka walked toward the water. "This is my Lava Dragon, Ka. We come from an island, too."

Tani's huge tail began to thrash back and forth in the waves. Droplets rained on Drake and the others.

Shu swiftly floated back to Bo.

Ka roared, and an orange light began to glow deep inside him.

"What's happening?" Drake asked.

Opeli placed a hand on her dragon. "What's wrong, Ka?"

Her Ahi Stone began to glow. "Ka remembers stories that his grandmother told him," she said. "Many, many years ago, there was a big fight between Lava Dragons and Sea Dragons. It happened when they both lived together on the islands of Noa."

"Tani says the same thing," Manawa said, his stone glowing as well. "The fight between the dragons lasted for many years. Finally, the Sea Dragons agreed to leave Noa. Today, they live in oceans all over the world. But they have never forgiven the Lava Dragons for making them leave the islands of Noa."

"Uh-oh," Drake said. "The last thing we need right now is a fight between dragons."

Opeli patted Ka's leg. "That was a long time ago. Can you and Tani find peace here today? We need to help Drake."

Ka's orange glow began to fade.

"That was a very nice way to calm him down," Bo said, and Opeli smiled.

Manawa turned to

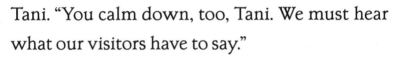

Tani. "You calm down, too, Tani. We must hear what our visitors have to say."

The Sea Dragon stopped thrashing.

"Manawa, we need your help," Drake said. "Like I said before, an evil wizard named Astrid is trying to cast a dangerous spell. We will need three dragons to break the spell. One of them is a Sea Dragon."

"We'd like you and Tani to come with us to the Kingdom of Bracken, where we live," Bo said. "Just for a little while."

Manawa frowned. "I don't know," he said. "I'm not —"

Suddenly, a big swirling portal of red light appeared on the beach!

ASTRID ATTACKS!

A red-headed wizard stepped out of the portal.

"Astrid!" Drake yelled.

"Tani, attack!" Manawa cried.

Drake spun around. "No!" he yelled. "Astrid can steal dragon powers!"

Manawa frowned as he held up a hand to stop Tani.

"That's right," Astrid said. The portal stayed in the air behind her, swirling. "And I will steal *all* your dragons' powers unless you give me what I want."

Drake's mind raced as he tried to figure out what to do.

"What do you want?" he asked, even though he knew.

"I want my branch from the shadow bush back, of course," she said.

"I left it in Bracken," Drake lied.

Astrid laughed. The sound reminded Drake of a cackling crow.

"Do you really think you can fool me, little boy?" she asked. "When you stole my branch, I asked my gazing ball to find it. I know it's here with you. Maybe a little truth spell will loosen your tongue."

She pointed at him. Red magic sparked from her fingertips.

Drake had an idea. He quickly stuck his hand in his pocket and felt for one of the thorns. Then he pressed his finger against it. "Ouch!"

"Drake!" Opeli cried.

Drake looked down at his body — and he couldn't see it! He could only see an outline of his body in shadow against the sand.

He heard Worm's voice in his head.

Run, Drake!

Drake ran. He ran across the cove into the trees and plants. Then he hid behind a bush and held his breath.

"Very clever, Drake!" Astrid called out. "But I will get that branch from you. And when I do, you will stay a shadow forever!"

A HARD CHOICE

rake patted his arms and legs. *Weird! Even though I look like a shadow, I still feel solid*, he thought. *Now that Astrid can't see me, I need to do whatever I can to protect this branch!*

Then he heard Opeli.

"Ka, Astrid can steal your powers, but she can't steal your *strength*!" she yelled. "Knock that wizard down with your tail!"

"Good idea!" Bo cried. "Shu, help Ka. Just don't use your powers."

Astrid spun around and saw the Lava Dragon stomping toward her. Shu came from another direction, riding the air currents.

"You won't stop me so easily!" Astrid cried.
She raised her hands to start a magical attack.

Tani dived under the waves. Her tail shot up
out of the water, sending a foamy wave onto the
shore. It splashed on the dragons and knocked
Astrid off her feet.

Drake reached out to Worm with his mind.

Worm, if you can sense where I am, come find me, Drake said. *Transport us back to Bracken. We'll leave the branch there so it will be safe. Then we can return and help the others.*

I can find you, Worm replied, and he began to crawl across the sand.

But before Worm reached Drake, Astrid jumped to her feet. She floated in the air, away from Shu and Ka.

Astrid pointed at Manawa, Opeli, and Bo.

"You know how strong my magic is, Drake," she said. "Give me the branch. If you do not, I will zap your friends' Dragon Stones. They will no longer be able to control their dragons. I will attack the dragons, and they will use their powers to defend themselves. Then I will capture those powers!"

Drake froze. He knew what Astrid could do with stolen dragon powers. He had seen her breathe fire like a Fire Dragon. He had seen her turn living beings to stone like a Stone Dragon.

If I don't do what Astrid wants, it will be bad. She would have the powers of a Lava Dragon, a Sea Dragon, and a Water Dragon. He shivered, thinking about all the damage Astrid could do.

If I give her the branch from the shadow bush, she'll leave us alone, Drake thought. *But then she'll also be able to finish the False Life spell. What should I do?*

TRICKED!

rake stepped out into the open. His shadow moved across the sand.

"How can I trust you?" Drake asked the wizard.

Astrid located the sound of his voice. Her eyes fixed on his shadow. "Give me the branch," she said as she floated over to the still-swirling portal. "I'll go right back to Navid and finish my spell."

Drake took a deep breath. *I hate to give up the branch*, he thought. *But it's the only way to stop Astrid from hurting more of my friends.*

He reached for the branch inside his pocket. He knew what he needed to do. Drake bit his lip and pressed his finger against a thorn.

Instantly, Drake could see himself again. He was no longer a shadow.

He walked up to Astrid. "Here you go," he said, holding the branch up to her.

She took it from him and tucked it into her belt. A huge grin spread across her face.

"Oh, you sweet, trusting boy," she said. Magical energy crackled from her fingertips.

Astrid pointed at Bo. Red light streaked from her fingertips and hit the boy's Dragon Stone. The stone turned black.

Zap! Zap! She hit Opeli's and Manawa's Ahi Stones next. They turned black, too.

She lied! Drake thought. *I can't let her zap my Dragon Stone! I don't think Worm would use his powers without me, but I can't take that chance.* He ran back into the trees.

Astrid grabbed an empty bottle from her belt.

"Now I will attack your dragons, and they will attack me back!" she cried, cackling with laughter. "Then I will steal their powers!"

Manawa sprang forward.

"No, you won't!" he yelled.

Manawa pushed Astrid as hard as he could. Then he thudded back onto the sand.

Astrid's mouth opened in shock as she fell backward into the portal.

"Noooooooooooooooo!" she wailed.

FIRE AND WATER

The portal closed. The evil wizard was gone.

Drake ran over and helped Manawa to his feet.

"Manawa, that was awesome!" Drake said.

Manawa grinned. "Thanks," he said.

"Yes, you stopped Astrid from stealing our dragons' powers," Bo said. "But now that she has the branch, she can cast the False Life spell."

Drake nodded. "I know. It was a hard choice, and I'm sorry I trusted her," he said. "What did she do to your stones? They're black."

Opeli closed her eyes. Then she opened them. "My Ahi Stone doesn't seem to work. I can't hear Ka in my head."

"And I can't hear Tani," Manawa replied.

"I can't hear Shu, either," Bo said. "Shu, can you understand me when I speak? Nod your head if you can."

But Shu didn't nod.

"This is awful!" Drake cried.

"It is," Bo agreed. "There must be some way to —"

Raaaaaaaaawwwwwwr!

Ka let out a loud roar and stomped toward the ocean.

"Ka, no!" Opeli yelled, running after him.

Tani raised her head out of the water.

Manawa ran to the water's edge and waved his arms. "Be calm, Tani!" he begged.

Drake turned to Bo. "They remember the fight from long ago! Now that Manawa and Opeli can't keep them calm, Ka and Tani are going to battle!"

"No, Tani!" Manawa called out. "You do not need to fight this dragon."

Ka let out another earth-shattering roar. His body glowed orange, and he aimed a stream of hot lava at Tani. The Sea Dragon ducked under the waves.

Then Tani's head emerged, and her body glowed turquoise. A huge glowing wave rose up behind her and then splashed down on Ka.

"I can't stop Ka!" Opeli cried.

Manawa shook his fists. "Tani, listen to me!"

Ka stomped his feet, making the ground shake. White smoke poured from his nostrils. Lightning streaked the sky.

Opeli gasped. "This will sometimes happen when a volcano erupts!" she cried. "Before the lava pours out, the earth moves. And lightning flashes."

Ka reared his head back.

Raaaaaaaaaaaaawwwwwwr!

Ka spewed another stream of hot, bubbling lava from his mouth.

THEY WON'T LISTEN!

The boiling hot lava almost hit Tani, but the Sea Dragon dived under the water. The lava quickly cooled.

"Ka, enough!" Opeli cried. "Tani is not your enemy."

Ka roared again and stomped his feet.

Opeli shook her head. "He won't listen! He doesn't understand me."

"Tani doesn't understand me, either," Manawa said.

"Can I ask Worm to communicate with your dragons?" Drake asked.

"Let's see what Worm can do," Manawa replied.

Worm had heard Drake. *I will do my best*, he said. *I will begin with Tani.*

Worm moved close to the edge of the water. His body glowed green. Tani continued to duck and thrash.

She is very angry, Worm replied. *Tani says that Sea Dragons vowed to live in peace when they left the islands of Noa. She is angry with Ka for coming to this land. I cannot calm her. And she told me to tell you this is a matter between dragons, not humans.*

"Can't you tell her that Ka didn't come here to start trouble?" Drake asked.

Worm shook his head. *She is too angry to listen to reason.*

Drake looked out at the ocean. Tani had stopped thrashing. But her body was glowing turquoise. She swam away from the shore. The waves followed her, uncovering the sand below.

"Is she leaving?" Drake asked.

Manawa's eyes were wide. "No," he said. "She is preparing to use her strongest power. We are all in danger!"

SAVE THE VILLAGE!

hat power is Tani going to use?" Drake asked. He glanced at the ocean. He had never seen it do this before. The water pulled farther and farther from the land.

"The *ngaru nui*," Manawa said. "A very, very big wave."

"We call it a tidal wave on my island," Opeli added. "A wave so big it can wipe out a village. Or even an island."

Manawa nodded. "Yes."

Manawa pointed to the hill. "The village is that way. Warn my people. Tell them to get to higher ground."

"Everyone, touch Worm!" Drake cried. "We can get there quickly."

"I must stay here," Manawa said. "It is my sworn duty to protect Tani — and to protect others *from* Tani. I need to keep trying to connect with her."

"I must stay as well," Opeli replied. "I am responsible for Ka."

"But, Manawa and Opeli —" Drake began.

Manawa shook his head. "Just go, and save my village!"

"Hurry! The wave is coming. There is no time!" Opeli cried.

An enormous wave was heading toward the shore. It glowed with Tani's turquoise light. The wave looked to Drake as tall as King Roland's castle!

"Bo, touch Worm and Shu!" Drake said, and Bo quickly obeyed. Drake put a hand on his dragon. "Now, Worm, transport us to the village!"

Worm transported them right away. They landed in a village filled with huts that reminded Drake of his village in Bracken. The villagers gathered around Drake, Bo, and their dragons.

Pania pushed through the crowd. "See, I told you!" she said. "Baby dragons!"

Bo stepped forward. "A *ngaru nui* is coming!" he said. "We must head for the top of the hill — now!"

"Wait, where is Manawa?" Pania asked. "And your other friend, Opeli?"

Drake gazed out toward the ocean. He could see the enormous wave getting closer and closer. Manawa bravely stood on the rock with his hands on his hips. Opeli stood onshore, while Ka roared and stomped his feet on the sand.

Worm, we have to get them to safety, Drake said.

I know, Worm agreed.

"Bo, we'll be right back," Drake said. "Help the villagers get away!"

Then Drake touched his dragon, and they transported back down to the shore.

THE BIG WAVE

rake and Worm landed on the shore next to Opeli and Ka. The sound of the approaching wave roared louder than any dragon.

"Manawa, get down! Both of you, touch Worm!" Drake yelled over the roar of the wave. "We have to get out of here!"

Suddenly, Worm's body began to glow. He moved away from the Dragon Masters and faced the tidal wave.

"Worm, what are you doing?" Drake cried.

The glow exploded from Worm's body in a shower of green light. The light hit the bright turquoise wall of water.

The wave began to glow with Worm's light. Then the wave stopped moving. It broke up into tiny droplets. The sparkly blue-green water rained down like mist all over the island.

"You saved us, Worm!" Drake yelled.

The glow faded from Worm's body, and the dragon collapsed on the sand. Drake ran to his side. Worm opened his eyes.

"Worm, are you okay?" Drake asked.

I am fine, Worm replied. *Just weak.*

"Thank you, Worm," Manawa said. Then he gazed out at the ocean.

Waves peacefully lapped against the shore. Tani bobbed on top of the water.

"She is calm for now," he said, looking down at his black Ahi Stone. "But how long will this peace last?"

Ka was still stomping his feet on the shore. A wisp of white smoke came from his nostrils.

"That wet mist cooled Ka down," Opeli said. "But he's about to get angry again."

Bo ran down to the beach. Shu flew behind him.

"That was amazing!" Bo cried. "And seeing Worm's mist gave me an idea. Shu's blue mist can heal dark magic."

"That's right!" Drake said.

"I think she can turn our stones back on," Bo said. "Drake, can you ask Worm to explain to Shu what we need her to do?"

"I will," Drake said. He closed his eyes and repeated Bo's idea to Worm.

Worm still looked weak. But the Earth Dragon nodded and closed his eyes. His body glowed green as he communicated with Shu.

"Manawa, Opeli, stand next to me!" Bo cried, and the two Dragon Masters ran to join him.

A moment later, Shu's body began to glow a soft blue. She opened her mouth, and a pale, misty blue cloud came out.

CHAPTER 14

PEACE AT LAST?

Shu's blue cloud floated through the air. Her healing mist rained down on the three black stones.

I hope this works! Drake thought.

The black slowly faded from the stones. Within seconds, the stones returned to their original green.

"Thank you, Shu!" Bo said, patting his dragon.

A moment later, Bo's Dragon Stone glowed brightly.

He smiled. "Shu can understand me!"

Opeli's Ahi Stone began to glow, and so did Manawa's.

"I can hear Ka in my head again!" Opeli said, smiling. "He said he missed being connected to me."

"I can hear Tani, too," Manawa announced. "She did not like being without a Dragon Friend, either."

He turned to Drake. "You have helped my people. I would like to help you stop that wizard."

"Thank you!" Drake said.

Manawa frowned. "But I worry that — even with our stones working again — it is too dangerous for Tani and Ka to be together. How can Opeli and I help you if we are always trying to keep our dragons calm?" he asked.

"It is time for them to make peace," Opeli said. "Ka, come."

Opeli and Ka walked to the water's edge, and Manawa followed them. Tani calmly floated on the water near the shore.

Opeli and Ka slowly approached the Sea Dragon.

Then she stopped and turned to Manawa. "Please tell Tani that Ka and I did not come here to challenge her," Opeli said. "We came to ask for help. Help to stop the evil wizard who made our stones go black."

Manawa's Ahi Stone glowed as he repeated this to Tani.

Opeli looked at Ka. "Will you keep the peace with Tani while we fight the wizard?"

Ka roared, and Opeli smiled. "He said yes!"

"Tani, Ka will not fight you. Will you promise to do the same?" Manawa asked.

The Sea Dragon nodded her shaggy head.

"There will be no more fighting!" Manawa announced.

Opeli smiled. She climbed onto Ka's tail. Her Ahi Stone glowed.

Ka lifted his tail over the water. Opeli reached out and touched Tani's face.

"Thank you," she said.

"This is great!" Drake said. "Now we should hurry and get back to Bracken. We'll need both your dragons to reverse Astrid's terrible spell!"

WHAT'S WRONG, WORM?

"Manawa! You're okay!" Pania cried.

She ran onto the beach and hugged her brother. Several villagers streamed behind her. A man and woman emerged from the crowd and approached Manawa.

"Mother! Father!" Manawa cried. "So much has happened. An evil wizard took away the power of my Ahi Stone. Tani created a *ngaru nui*. And this dragon, Worm, saved us all."

He pointed to Worm, who was still curled up on the sand.

Drake stepped forward. "I'm Drake, Worm's Dragon Master. We need Manawa and Tani to come with us to help us defeat the wizard."

Manawa's father nodded. "As a Dragon Friend, Manawa must protect the world from evil."

Manawa's mother hugged him. "How long will you be gone?"

"Just a few days," Drake replied. "We can get to my land, Bracken, quickly. And then we need to find one more dragon and create the counterspell."

Drake turned to Manawa. "To transport to Bracken, we all need to be connected to Worm. You just need to touch Worm with one hand and Tani with the other. Can she leave the ocean?"

Manawa nodded. "She can." His Ahi Stone glowed, and Tani crawled onto the shore. Drake's eyes widened as he took in the huge size of the Sea Dragon.

Some villagers had approached Worm and were gently petting and thanking him. Worm was sitting up, and he looked better.

"Can you please transport us to the Valley of Clouds?" Drake asked. "I'm not sure Tani will fit inside the castle."

Worm nodded.

Drake touched Worm. "Ready!" he said.

Worm began to glow a very soft green. Drake closed his eyes, preparing to transport.

Nothing happened. He opened his eyes. Worm's glow had faded.

"Worm, what's wrong?" Drake asked his tired-looking dragon.

I am too weak, Worm replied. *I cannot transport!*

A FEAST

"Oh no!" Drake cried. "Nothing like this has ever happened before!"

"Is Worm all right?" Bo asked.

"I'm not sure," Drake said.

"How are you feeling?" Drake asked Worm.

Tired, Worm replied. *But I think I am getting stronger.*

Just then, Drake remembered the magic mirror. "Let me ask Griffith if there's anything he can do."

Drake took the mirror off his belt. He looked into it.

"Griffith, are you there?" he asked.

The glass in the mirror swirled, and the wizard's face appeared. "Drake! Have you found the Sea Dragon?"

"Yes," Drake said. "But a lot of things have happened."

Drake told Griffith everything.

"And now Astrid has the branch from the shadow bush," Drake finished. "And Worm can't transport."

"Worm must have used a lot of power to stop that tidal wave," Griffith said. "He just needs to rest. And don't worry about the branch. Because you took it from Astrid while she was casting the spell, she will have to start the spell all over again. We have a few days. Rest and return when you are ready."

"We will," Drake promised, and Griffith's face faded.

Drake looked up to see everyone gathered around him — the other Dragon Masters and the villagers.

Manawa put an arm around Drake. "We will take care of you," he promised. "Let's go to the village!"

Then Manawa turned to Tani. "You may go back to the sea for now, my friend. I will see you later!"

Tani nodded and returned to the ocean.

The villagers led the way back up the hill. Worm moved slowly, and Drake stayed with him the whole way.

Once they got to the village, Manawa put a hand on Worm. "This is Worm, the dragon who saved us!" he announced. "He needs food and rest!"

"What does he eat?" Pania asked Drake.

"He likes all kinds of fruit," Drake replied. "And vegetables."

Pania ran off and came back with two girls her age, carrying baskets of large orange berries. They placed them in front of Worm, and he gobbled them up.

Nearby, smoke was coming from a pit dug into the ground. Delicious smells began to fill the air.

"Is that food cooking?" Bo asked.

Manawa nodded. "It's fish. With orange yams. And the white vegetable is taro root."

"It smells delicious!" Drake said, and Manawa nodded.

When the food was ready, the villagers and Dragon Masters feasted. Drake ate every tasty bite.

After the feast, the dragons slept on beds of grass that the villagers had made for them.

Manawa's parents set up sleeping mats for Drake, Bo, and Opeli in their home. A full belly helped Drake fall into a deep sleep.

He awoke to sun streaming into the hut — and to Griffith's voice.

"Drake, are you there? I have news!" Griffith said.

Drake grabbed the mirror. "I'm here!"

"Rori and Ana learned where to find a Wind Dragon," Griffith told him. "That is good news. But I have bad news, too."

"What bad news?" Drake asked.

"We got a report from wizards in Navid," Griffith replied. "Astrid is using more powerful magic than they have ever seen. She has sped up the False Life spell. She is about to bring the bones to life!"

Drake jumped up. "Everyone, Astrid is about to cast her spell!" he cried. "I hope Worm is ready to transport. We need to get back to Bracken and find a Wind Dragon right away!"

TRACEY WEST is a *New York Times* bestselling children's book author. She likes to swim in the ocean and has seen many jellyfish, but no Sea Dragons there.

Tracey is the stepmom to three grown-up kids. She shares her home with her husband, dogs, chickens, and a garden full of worms. They live in the misty mountains of New York State, where it is easy to imagine dragons roaming free in the green hills.

MATT LOVERIDGE loves illustrating children's books. When he's not painting or drawing, he likes hiking, biking, and drinking milk right from the carton. He lives in the mountains of Utah with his wife and kids, and their black dog named Blue.

DRAGON MASTERS
WAVE OF THE SEA DRAGON

Questions and Activities

Drake steals Astrid's branch from a shadow bush. Why is this branch dangerous? Why does Astrid come after Drake for it instead of collecting a new one? Reread Chapter 3.

When Tani and Ka first meet on page 33, they start to attack each other. Why?

Manawa and Opeli are easily able to calm Tani and Ka on page 36. Why are they unable to calm their dragons across Chapters 10–13?

In this fictional story, the Sea Dragon creates a tidal wave. But tidal waves can happen in the real world. Research *tidal waves*. Then write and draw what you learn about them.

Stealing and lying are often the actions of a bad character. But Drake does both in this book. Do you think Drake's behavior is okay? Explain your answer.